Project Director and Head of Publications, NMAI:
    Terence Winch
Photo and Research Editor, NMAI: Lou Stancari
Editor, NMAI: Cheryl Wilson
Executive Editor, Abbeville: Nancy Grubb
Designer, Abbeville: Molly Shields
Production Editor, Abbeville: Meredith Wolf Schizer
Production Manager, Abbeville: Lou Bilka

For information about the National Museum of the American
Indian, visit the NMAI Website at www.si.edu/nmai.

PHOTOGRAPHY CREDITS
Pam Dewey: p. 30 top right; Carmelo Guadagno: p. 29
bottom right; David Heald: p. 30 top left and bottom left;
Fred Meyer: p. 31 top right; Fred E. Miller: p. 31 bottom right;
Willem Wildschut: p. 29 bottom left and p. 31 top left.

First edition
10 9 8 7 6 5 4 3 2 1

Library of Congress Cataloging-in-Publication Data
Medicine Crow, Joseph, 1913–
    Brave Wolf and the Thunderbird : tales of the people /
story by Joe Medicine Crow ; illustrations by Linda R. Martin.
        p.   cm.
    Summary: While hunting, Brave Wolf is snatched by a
huge Thunderbird and taken to her nest on a high cliff so he
can protect her chicks from a monster.
    ISBN 0-7892-0160-7
    1. Crow Indians–Folklore.   2. Tales–Montana.   3.
Thunderbird (Legendary character)–Legends.   [1. Thunderbird
(Legendary character)–Legends.   2. Crow Indians–Folklore.   3.
Indians of North America–Montana–Folklore.   4. Folklore–
Montana.]   I. Martin, Linda R., ill.   II. Title.
E99.C92M4 1998
398.2′0899752–DC21   98-5294

The National Museum of the American Indian, Smithsonian Institution, is dedicated to working in
collaboration with the indigenous peoples of the Americas to protect and foster Native cultures
throughout the Western Hemisphere. The museum's publishing program seeks to augment awareness
of Native American beliefs and lifeways, and to educate the public about the history and
significance of Native cultures.
    The museum's George Gustav Heye Center in Manhattan opened in 1994; its Cultural
Resources Center opens in Suitland, Maryland, in 1998; in 2002, the museum will open its primary
facility on the National Mall in Washington.

BRAVE WOLF and the THUNDERBIRD

Story by Joe Medicine Crow
Illustrations by Linda R. Martin

Tales of the People

National Museum of the American Indian,
Smithsonian Institution
Washington, D.C., and New York

Abbeville Press   Publishers
New York   London   Paris

One day, a man named Brave Wolf went hunting in the hills. He did not return for several weeks, and when he came back to camp, he told his family and friends what had happened to him while he was gone.

7

While he was hunting, a huge Thunderbird flew over and snatched him up in her giant claws. She took him to a high cliff, overlooking a lake up in the mountains.

9

There on the cliff was a nest with two chicks, just beginning to get big. The mother Thunderbird said to Brave Wolf, "I have brought you up here for a purpose. In the spring, when my young ones are just about so big, a monster comes out of the water in that lake down there and climbs up this cliff to eat my little ones. It's been doing that for quite a while.

"I've tried everything to stop that monster. I've hit it with my lightning, but I can't stop it. So now I have brought you, a human being, to come help me."

"All right," said Brave Wolf, "let me think about it and see what I can do."

After Brave Wolf thought for a while, he said to the Thunderbird, "Go out and get me some dry logs. I want to build a fire." The Thunderbird took off, and pretty soon she came back with a dried log and some branches and stacked them in a pile.

"Now," he said, "I'll need some nice round rocks." So the Thunderbird went off and brought some back, and soon Brave Wolf had a big pile of rocks.

13

"Next," Brave Wolf said, "I will need you to kill a large buffalo and bring it here." The Thunderbird did as he asked. Brave Wolf skinned the buffalo, and from the hide he made a basket that would hold water. The Thunderbird used the rest of the buffalo to feed her chicks.

"All right," Brave Wolf said, "I'll need water. Let me know when you think the monster is going to rise out of the lake. That's when I'll need the water."

After a while, the Thunderbird noticed that waves were building on the lake, and she told Brave Wolf, "The monster is coming up in about a day."

Then the Thunderbird caused a quick little rain shower that filled Brave Wolf's basket with water.

17

Brave Wolf built a fire right near the edge of the cliff, just where the monster would come up, and he heated the rocks in the fire.

The monster was a great big snake, something like a dragon. It started rising up out of the lake, and the waves got higher and higher.

21

When the monster started climbing the cliff, the
Thunderbird flew down and struck it with lightning.
But she couldn't stop it. It kept coming up slowly,
slowly, slowly, getting pretty close to the top.
And when it got to the top, the monster opened
its mouth.

Brave Wolf was ready. He had made a couple of big forks out of tree limbs so he could push the burning rocks into the monster's mouth. He kept throwing in those red-hot rocks, and when the monster had swallowed them all, Brave Wolf poured the water from his basket into its mouth. Steam shot up and made all kinds of hissing noises. The monster started wobbling around, groaning, and finally it fell backward into the lake with a big splash.

And that was the end of the monster.

25

The Thunderbird invited all the birds of the country to come have a big feast. They came and ate the monster—ate it all up!

And then, the Thunderbird carried Brave Wolf back home.

The Thunderbird

Many Native American cultures tell stories of supernatural creatures. Birds with black feathers, giant wingspans, and two sharp claws are found in Crow and Blackfoot lore. Crow legends tell of Sua'dagagay—the Thunderbird—a creature so strong it can carry off huge animals in its talons. (In the Crow language, *sua* means thunder, *dagagay* means bird.) Crow people regard the Thunderbird as the most powerful of all spirits.

Kwagu'ł (Kwakiutl) housefront with Thunderbird design. P8907.
Native buildings often reflect the beliefs and traditions of the community. This Kwagu'ł (Kwakiutl) housefront is painted with a stylized design depicting Thunderbird carrying a whale in its talons. It probably represents the family's ancestral heritage or clan.

The Crows say that lightning bolts shoot from the eyes of the Thunderbird, and that when the Thunderbird flaps its wings and blinks its eyes, storms rage and rain pours down. Severe damage is sometimes caused by lightning from young, mischief-making Thunderbirds, but old Thunderbirds are wise and never kill anybody. They protect the people who believe in them, offering brotherhood, peace, plenty, and goodwill.

Peoples of the Great Plains call thunder beings *wakinyan*, or "sacred flying ones." The Haida, Tlingit, and Quileute of the Northwest Coast have legends of a whale-eating Thunderbird. The Quileute say that long ago, when a period of harsh weather killed the edible plants and prevented the men from fishing, the Great Spirit saved the people by sending Thunderbird, in whose great claws dangled a giant, living whale. The huge bird, with wings twice as long as a war canoe, carefully lowered the whale to the people, thus sparing them from starvation.

Decorated Absaroke (Crow) tipi. Montana. N21057.
Tipis, shirts, and robes were sometimes painted with designs illustrating clan symbols or spirit beings—such as Thunderbird—or depicting scenes of military accomplishment.

Glossary of Crow Words

boy	*cikyá.ke*
girl	*bi.akà.te*
man	*batsé*
buffalo	*bicé* or *be=shá*
horse	*itsí.re*
Thunderbird	*suá'dagagay*
water monster	*buruksá.m wurukcé*
fire	*ambiré* or *birá*
lake	*birítsgyé*
water	*biré*

Absaroke (Crow) children. P4231.

These children grew up at a time when making things—household goods, hunting equipment, religious objects, and clothing—was a never-ending part of daily Crow life.

Spotted Rabbit, Absaroke (Crow). Montana. N13765.

Traditional Crow clothing incorporated painted images from dreams and visions in tribute to spirit forces. Designs were made using beads obtained through trade, dyed porcupine quills, and pigments applied with porous buffalo bones. Headgear was often decorated with eagle feathers, which were sacred to the Crow.

Absaroke (Crow) hide effigy of an elk. 9 x 6⁷/₈ x ¹/₄ in. (23 x 17.5 x .5 cm). 15.3260.

The elk held great significance for Plains people. Effigies such as this may have been created to reflect the elk's importance or to embody its power or spirit.

The Crow People

In their own language, Crows are called *Absaroke*, which means Children of the Large-Beaked Bird. Other Native cultures referred to the Absaroke as the "Sharp People," meaning that they were as crafty and alert as the *absa,* or raven.

Hand signs were a common form of communication among peoples of the Plains. The Absaroke used a hand sign that looked like the flapping of a bird's wings as the sign for their tribe. Early non-Natives interpreted the hand sign as a crow and called the people the Crow Indians.

Originally from the forests of the Northeast, the tribe consists of two main bands: the River Crows, who by the 1800s lived along the Missouri, Milk, and Yellowstone Rivers in Montana and Wyoming, and the Mountain Crows, who settled along the high mountains of northern Wyoming and southern Montana. A third, smaller group, known as the Kicked-in-the-Bellies, was closely related to the Mountain Crows.

Today the Crow Indian Reservation— nearly two and a half million acres of mountains, foothills, and plains—is located southeast of Billings, Montana, within boundaries defined in 1885. More than six thousand people live in Crow territory in Montana.

Absaroke (Crow) sword scabbard, late 19th century. Montana. Beaded rawhide stitched with buckskin cord and edged with flannel, 52⁷/8 x 25¹/4 in. (134 x 64 cm). 8480.

Absaroke (Crow) hide mirror case with beaded decoration. Montana. 31⁷/8 x 6⁵/8 x ⁵/8 in. (81 x 17 x 1.5 cm). 23.2178.

Absaroke (Crow) horsegear. Montana. Painted hide, 25 x 30¹/8 in. (63.2 x 76.2 cm). 18.9233.